The Fisherman and His Wife

by the Brothers Grimm, translated by Elizabeth Shub, illustrated by Monika Laimgruber

Greenwillow Books, A Division of William Morrow & Company, Inc., New York

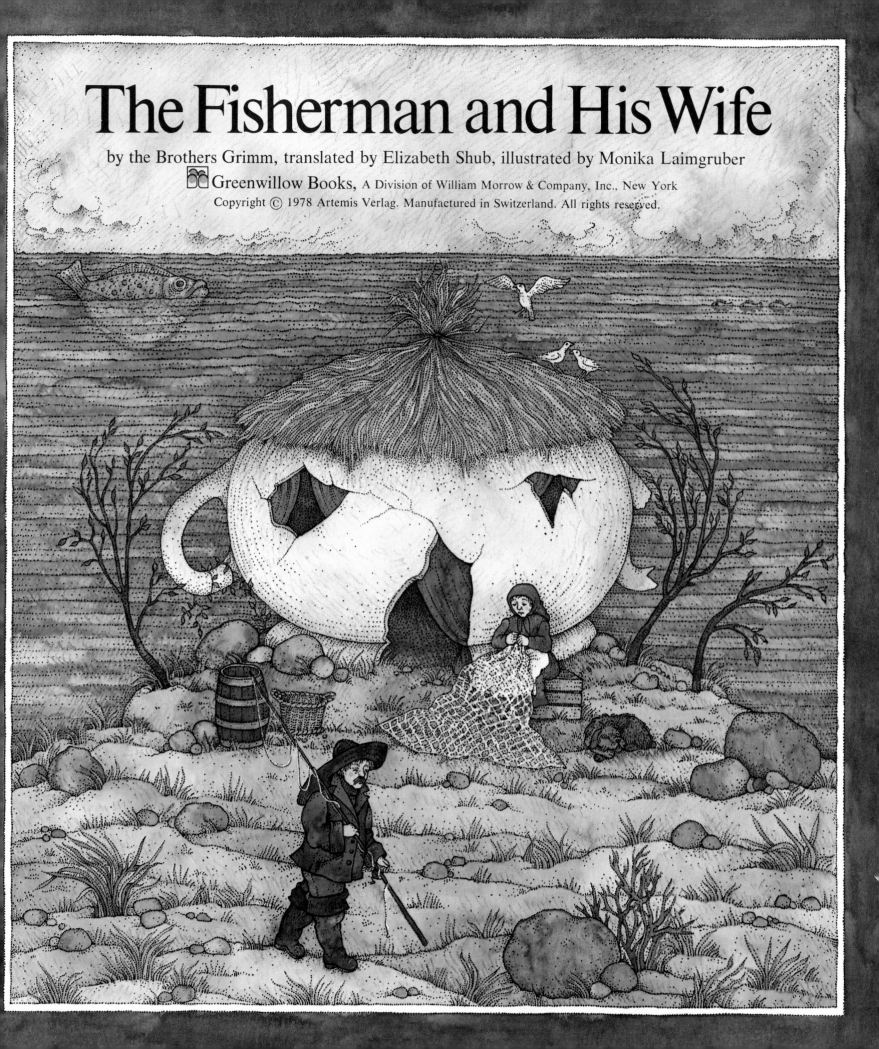

There was once a fisherman who lived with his
wife in a night pot near the sea. Each day he went
fishing. He fished and he fished.

One day as he sat angling and staring into the clear
water, sat and sat, he felt a sudden tug on his line.
When he hauled it up, there was a large flounder
at the end of it. The flounder said, "Look here,
fisherman, let me live. I am not a flounder but a
prince who has been enchanted. What good will it
do you to kill me? I won't even taste good. Put me
back into the water and let me swim away."

"Why talk so much?" said the fisherman. "I'd set
any speaking flounder free." And he put the
flounder back into the water. The flounder dove
to the ocean bed, leaving a long streak of blood
behind him.

The fisherman went home to his wife.

"Husband," said she, "haven't you brought home any fish today?"

"No," said he. "I did catch a flounder, but he said he was an enchanted prince and so I let him go."

"Did you make a wish?" said she.

"No," said he. "What should I have wished for?"

"It's so terrible to live here in this disgusting night pot. You might have wished for a nice little cottage. Go back and tell the flounder we want a nice little cottage. He'll give it to us."

"Oh," said the fisherman. "I can't go back and ask him now."

"Yes, you can," said she. "You caught the flounder, and you let him go free. Just go and ask him. Go right now!"

The fisherman didn't much like the idea, but neither did he want to argue with his wife, and so he went back to the sea. When he got there, he saw that the water had changed colour. It had turned green and yellow and was not nearly as clear as it had been. He stood on the shore and called:

"Flounder, flounder, in the sea,
Hear my words and come to me.
Grant the wish of Ilsebill,
Though her wish is not my will."

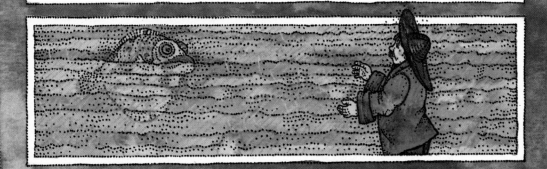

The flounder swam up and said, "Well, what does she want?"

"My wife says that when I set you free, I should have made a wish," said the fisherman. "She doesn't want to live in a night pot any longer. She'd like a little cottage."

"Go home," said the flounder. "She has it."

The fisherman went home. The night pot was gone. In its place stood a small cottage, and his wife sat on a bench in front of it. She got up, took him by the hand, and said, "Come on in and have a look. You'll see how much nicer this is."

Inside was a small entrance hall that led into a splendid little parlour. There was a bedroom with a bed in it, and there was a kitchen and pantry, equipped with dishes, the finest utensils, and beautifully polished pewter and brass—everything that might be needed. In back of the cottage was a small yard for the chickens and geese, and a small garden planted with vegetables and fruit trees.

"Look around," said she. "It is really nice."

"Yes," said he. "Now we can live here and be content." Then they had a bite to eat and went to bed.

All went well for a fortnight or so, when the wife said: "Listen, husband. We're so cramped here in this little cottage. And the yard and garden are so small. The flounder could just as well have given us a larger house. I'd like to live in a big stone castle. Go to the flounder and tell him to give us a castle."

"But, wife," said the fisherman, "this cottage is just right. Why would we want to live in a castle?"

"Stop talking nonsense," said she. "There's still time. Go to the flounder and ask him for a castle."

"No," said the fisherman. "The flounder gave us this nice cottage, I don't want to ask him for anything more. He may get annoyed."

"But it's no trouble for him. Why, he'll be glad to do it " said she. "Just go and ask him."

The fisherman's heart was heavy. He did not want to go. It's not right, he said to himself, but he went just the same.

When he came to the sea, he saw that the water was no longer green and yellow. It had turned purple, dark blue, and grey, and was murky. He stood on the shore and called:

> "Flounder, flounder, in the sea,
> Hear my words and come to me.
> Grant the wish of Ilsebill,
> Though her wish is not my will."

"Well, what does she want?" said the flounder.

"Oh dear," said the fisherman unhappily. "She wants to live in a castle."

"Go home. You'll find her standing at the door," said the flounder.

The fisherman set off for home, but when he arrived, there stood a large stone palace in place of the cottage and his wife was waiting on the steps. She took him by the hand and said, "Let's go in."

Inside was a long, marble-floored hall. As they walked along, footmen opened the heavy doors that led from room to room. The walls were hung with beautiful tapestries and all the rooms were furnished with chairs and tables of gold. The floors were covered with rugs and the tables were so heavily laden, they looked as if they might collapse under the weight of food and wine. In the large yard behind the palace there were stables to house the horses and handsome carriages, and barns for the cattle. There was also a magnificent garden with beautiful flowers, and trees bearing delicious fruits, and a park half a mile long where stags, does, and rabbits roamed about—everything that one could wish for.

"Now then," said the fisherman's wife, "isn't this nice?"

"Yes, indeed," said the fisherman. "We will live in this palace and be satisfied."

"We'll think about that," said she. "We'll sleep on it." And they went to bed.

The next morning the wife was the first to awake. It was dawn, and from her bed, through the window, she could see the beautiful countryside stretching far into the distance. The fisherman was still yawning as she poked him in the side with her elbow and said, "Husband, look out of the window. Why can't we be king of all this land? Go to the flounder and tell him we want to be king."

"But, wife," said the fisherman, "why king? I don't want to be king."

"Very well," said she. "If you don't want to be king, I'll be king. Go to the flounder and tell him."

"But, wife," said the fisherman, "why do you want to be king? I don't want to ask the flounder for that."

"Why not?" said she. "Go at once! I must be king."

The fisherman set off, but was most unhappy that his wife wanted to be king.

That is not right, that is not right, he thought, and he did not want to go. But he went nevertheless.

And when he came to the sea, he saw that it was slate grey and the churning water smelled foully. He stood on the shore and called:

"Flounder, flounder, in the sea,
   Hear my words and come to me.
   Grant the wish of Ilsebill,
   Though her wish is not my will."

"Well, what does she want?" said the flounder.

"She wants to be king," said the fisherman.

"Go home," said the flounder. "She is king."

The fisherman went home, and when he came to the palace, he found that it had grown much larger. A high tower had been added to it, as well as many ornaments. A sentry stood before the gate and a military band was playing. Inside the palace everything was of marble and gold. The satin draperies were tied back with thick gold-tasselled cord. As the fisherman reached the salon, the doors were thrown open. The entire court was gathered there and his wife sat on a high throne of gold and diamonds. She wore a tall golden crown on her head and in her hand was a sceptre of solid gold and precious stones. On either side of her, six gentlewomen stood lined up, each a head shorter than the one behind her. The fisherman stood before his wife and said, "Well, wife, are you now king?"

"Yes," said she. "I am king."

The fisherman stood there for a while, just looking at her. Then he said, "How fine it is that you are king. Now we don't need to wish for anything more."

"No, husband," said she impatiently. "I'm so bored. I can't stand it any more. I must be emperor."

"But, wife," said the fisherman, "why do you want to be emperor?"

"Husband," said she, "go to the flounder. Tell him I wish to be emperor."

"Wife," said the fisherman, "the flounder can't make you emperor. I won't ask him for that. There is only one emperor in the land. The flounder can't make you emperor. He cannot!"

"What!" said she. "I am king and you are only my husband. Go to the flounder this very minute. If he can make a king, he can make an emperor. It is my wish, and I will be emperor. Go!"

And so the fisherman was forced to go.

On the way, he grew more and more worried. He thought to himself, This can't end well. To want to be emperor is shameless. The flounder will surely have had enough.

When the fisherman reached the sea, he saw that it was black and syrupy. The water boiled and bubbled. A sharp wind arose, whipping it into a whirlpool. The fisherman turned green. He stood on the shore and called:

"Flounder, flounder, in the sea,
   Hear my words and come to me.
   Grant the wish of Ilsebill,
   Though it is against my will."

"Well, what does she want?" said the flounder.

"Oh, flounder," said the fisherman, "she wants to be emperor."

"Go home," said the flounder. "She is emperor."

The fisherman went home, and when he arrived he saw a castle of polished marble, adorned with alabaster statues and gilded ornaments. Before the gate, soldiers paraded in review, led by a band blowing their trumpets and beating their drums. And within the castle, barons, counts, and dukes were the servants, and they opened the doors of solid gold for him. And there at last was his wife sitting on a throne wrought from a single piece of gold, and it was two miles high. She wore a crown three ells tall. It was set with diamonds and other sparkling stones. In one hand she held a sceptre, in the other the imperial orb. On either side of her, in pairs, stood her gentlemen-at-arms, each pair shorter than the one behind. They ranged in size from the largest giant two miles tall to the tiniest dwarf the size of a finger. And surrounding her were the nobles of the court.

The fisherman stood among them and said, "Wife, are you now emperor?"

"Yes," she replied. "I am emperor."

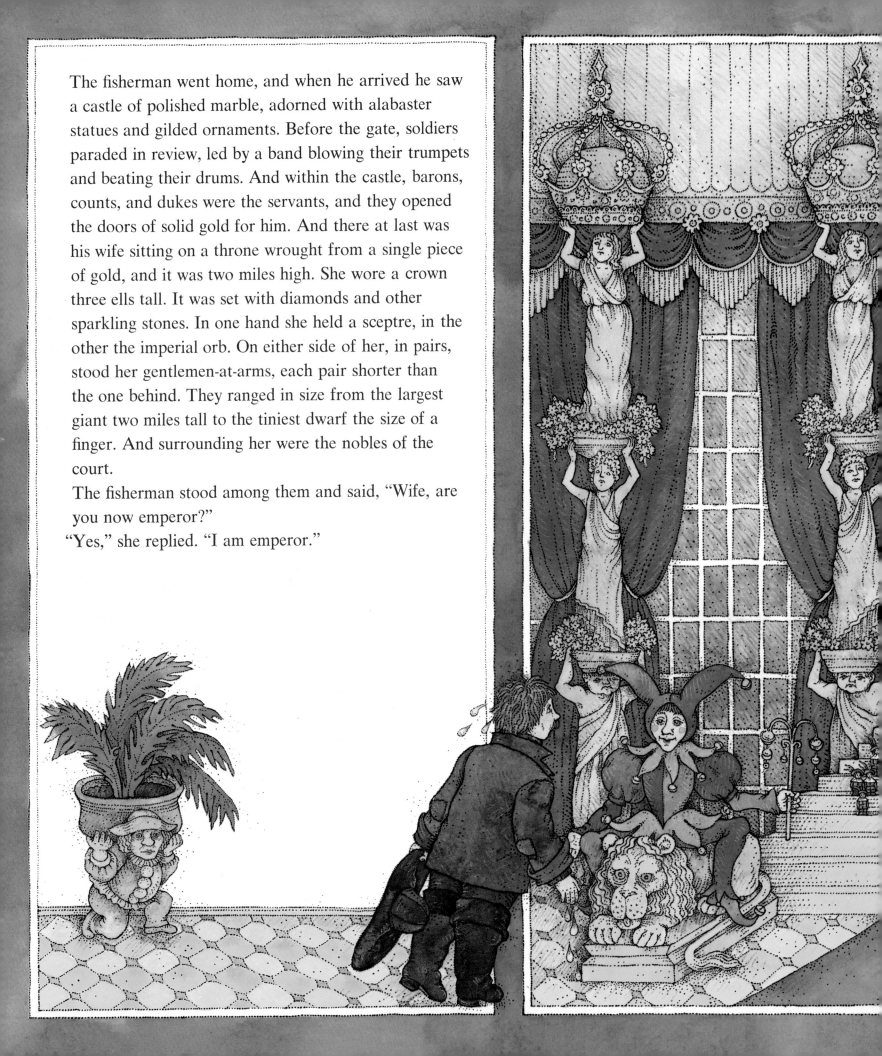

The fisherman stood there for a while taking it all in. Then he said, "How fine it is that you are emperor."

"Husband," said she, "what are you standing around for? I'm emperor, all right, but I want to be pope. Go to the flounder!"

"But, wife," said the fisherman, "what don't you want to be? You can't be pope. There is only one pope in Christendom. The flounder cannot make you pope."

"Husband," said she, "I want to be pope. Go at once. I must be pope before the day is out."

"No, wife," said he. "I don't want to ask the flounder for that. It won't end well. You're asking too much. The flounder cannot make you pope."

"Husband," said she, "will you stop jabbering? If the flounder can make an emperor, he can make a pope. Go to him at once! I am emperor and you are only my husband. On your way!"

The fisherman was afraid. He trembled and shook and he walked unsteadily, but he went. A mighty wind swept over the land, the clouds moved swiftly and it grew as dark as if night had come. The leaves were torn from the trees and the waves raged and roared and pounded the shore. In the distance, the fisherman saw ships in distress tossing on the water. In the middle of the sky, there was still a tiny patch of blue, but beyond it, the horizon was red with the threatening storm. The fisherman stood hopelessly on the shore and called:

> "Flounder, flounder, in the sea,
> Hear my words and come to me.
> Grant the wish of Ilsebill,
> Though it is against my will."

"Now then, what does she want?" said the flounder.

"She wants to be pope," said the fisherman.

"Go home. She is pope," said the flounder.

The fisherman went home, and when he got there, he saw a huge church surrounded by palaces. He forced his way through the crowd into the church. Thousands of candles lit the interior, and his wife, dressed all in gold cloth, sat on a throne even higher than the one she had as emperor. She wore three crowns on her head and she was surrounded by priestly dignitaries. On either side of her stood two rows of candles, the largest as thick and tall as a tower, the smallest, a tiny kitchen taper. Kings and princes kneeled at her feet and kissed her slippers.

"Wife," said the fisherman, and he gave her a searching look, "are you now pope?"

"Yes," she replied, "I am pope."

The fisherman looked squarely at her and it was as if he were looking into the sun. Then he said, "How fine it is that you are pope."

But she sat there as stiff as a tree trunk and did not move.

"Wife," the fisherman said, "now you must be satisfied, because you can't be more than pope."

"Well, I'll think about that," she said. Then they both went to bed. But greed kept her awake, and she thought about what else she might want to be. The fisherman had walked a lot that day and he slept soundly, though his wife tossed and turned the whole night long. Yet she could not think of what else to want.

Dawn came, and when she saw the red sunrise, she sat up in bed and stared at it. Then she thought, Why can't I make the sun and moon rise?

"Husband," she said, poking him in the ribs with her elbow, "wake up and go to the flounder. Tell him I want to be like God."

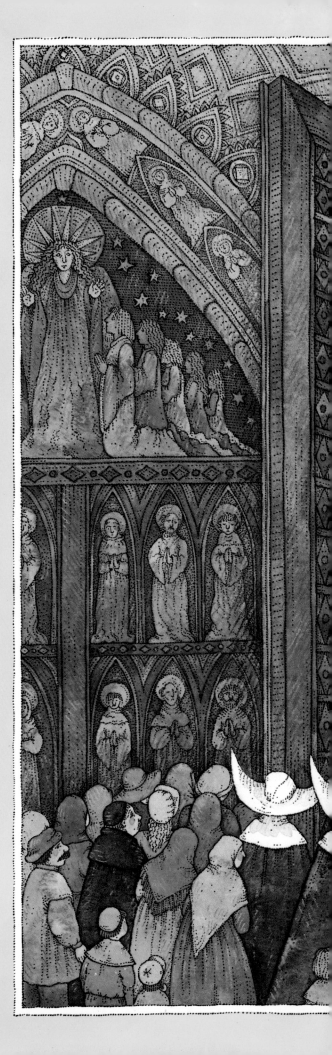

The fisherman was still half asleep, but she startled him so that he fell out of bed. He thought he was hearing things. He rubbed his eyes and said, "Now, wife, what did you say?"

"Husband," she said, "I can't stand just to look on when the sun and the moon rise. I won't have a peaceful hour unless I can be the one to make them do it."

She gave him such a terrifying look that he shuddered.

"Go at once to the flounder," she said. "Tell him I want to be like God."

"But, wife," the fisherman said and fell to his knees. "The flounder cannot do that. He can make an emperor, and a pope, but I beg of you, think it over, and be satisfied with being pope."

The fisherman's wife flew into a rage. She tossed her head in anger and her hair flew wildly about. She tore at her night dress. She kicked the fisherman and screeched, "I can't stand it, I can't stand it any longer. Will you go right now!"

The fisherman pulled on his trousers and ran off in a frenzy. Outside a storm raged, and he could hardly stay on his feet. Roofs were blown off and trees over-turned, the mountain quaked and chunks of cliff rolled into the sea. The sky was black as tar and it thundered and lightninged. The sea rose in frothing, mountainous waves as high as church towers.

The fisherman stood on the shore and shouted, but he could not hear himself:

> "Flounder, flounder, in the sea,
>   Hear my words and come to me.
>   Grant the wish of Ilsebill,
>   Though her wish is not my will."

"Now, what does she want?" said the flounder.

"She wants to be like God," said the fisherman.

"Go home," said the flounder. "You'll find her back in her night pot."

And there they are
to this very day.